·THE CHRONICLES OF·
NARNIA
THE LION, THE WITCH AND THE WARDROBE

Lucy's Adventure

HarperC

D0682482

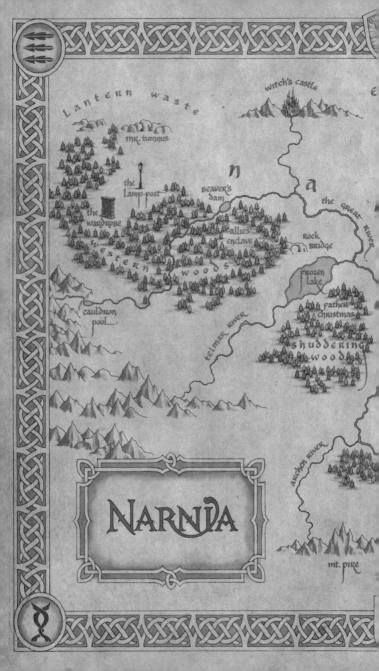

Lucy's Adventure: The Quest for Aslan, the Great Lion
text © 2005 C.S.Lewis Pte, Ltd

Photographs/art © 2005 Disney Enterprises, Inc.
and Walden Media, LLC

The Chronicles of Narnia®, Narnia® and all book titles, characters and locales
original to The Chronicles of Narnia are trademarks of C.S. Lewis Pte. Ltd.
Use without permission is strictly prohibited.

www.narnia.com

First published in Great Britain in 2005 by HarperCollins Children's Books.
HarperCollins Children's Books is a division
of HarperCollins Publishers Ltd.

1 3 5 7 9 10 8 6 4 2

0-00-773920-6

The HarperCollins website address is:
www.harpercollinschildrensbooks.co.uk

Printed and bound in Germany

Chapter One

Lucy Pevensie was only eight years old, but she still knew a lot of things. She wasn't completely sure why she was standing on the platform of a train station with her two brothers, Peter and Edmund and her sister Susan, but she knew it had something to do with the War. Daddy had gone to fight people called the Nazis, who were turning Europe into a horrible and dangerous place. Even though fighting is a bad thing to do, Lucy understood that it was important sometimes to fight to save and protect the innocent and the good. What Lucy didn't understand was why the Nazis were dropping bombs on people's houses in London and making her leave her mother behind and go into the countryside. That, Lucy couldn't understand.

As her mother hugged her, Lucy thought that it didn't seem very fair. If it wasn't safe for her and her brothers and sisters to live in London any more, then how could it be safe for their mother? Lucy grabbed hold of her elder brother Peter's hand. He was practically a grown-up like Mummy and Daddy anyway. As they stepped onto the train to take them to their new home, the home of Professor Kirke, Lucy turned to wave goodbye to her mother and watched sadly, as she followed the train down the platform.

The long train ride to the country ended at an empty platform. An old black buggy pulled up and a very stern woman got out. Lucy felt very small indeed under the woman's glare.

"Mrs... Macready?" Peter stammered.

"I'm afraid so," came the reply.

Lucy felt even smaller upon seeing the professor's mansion. As the others followed Mrs Macready down the hall, Lucy stopped. A light had just flickered behind a nearby door. Suddenly a shadow moved underneath it. Lucy gasped and dashed away to catch up with the others.

"The covers feel scratchy."

Lucy didn't like her new home. She didn't like the scary Mrs Macready who had met them at the train station. She didn't like the dark staircases. She didn't like the way floor felt cold and unfriendly underneath her bare feet. And she didn't like her new bed. The new bed was worst of all, but it wasn't really the covers that upset Lucy. It was the fact that her mother wasn't there to tuck her in at night and tell her everything was going to be okay.

Susan tried to comfort Lucy, "Wars don't last forever, Lucy. We'll be home soon."

"If home's still there," replied Edmund.

This was too much for Lucy. She didn't want to think of her lovely home being turned into a pile of burnt bricks. Lucy felt tears in her eyes.

Peter smiled and tried to cheer them all up. "Tomorrow's going to be great."

But it wasn't great at all. It was just very, very, very rainy.

Inside, all four children were bored. Susan was trying to make them play a dictionary game. Lucy loved her sister but thought that sometimes she could be a bit boring. Susan didn't seem to like outdoor games, but Lucy loved them. She liked running around and playing the games her brothers played. She wasn't afraid of exploring in forests or climbing trees or going to strange places.

"We could play hide and seek," Lucy suggested.

"Hide and seek's for children," Edmund said. He was only a little older than Lucy, and always tried to act more grown up than he was. Lucy didn't mind. She knew that Peter would play. Peter sighed and looked up into Lucy's pleading face. "One," he said slowly. "Two. Three."

Lucy darted away.

Dashing towards the windows, Lucy ripped back a heavy velvet curtain.

"I was here first," Edmund said, snapping the curtain back into place. Hurrying down the hall, Lucy came to a closed door.

"Eighty-nine," Peter said.

Quickly, Lucy shoved open the door and went inside. The room was empty except for a large wardrobe that sat against the wall. She hurried over to it and yanked on the knob. Taking a deep breath, Lucy dived into the wardrobe.

Inside, it was dark and surprisingly cold, as if there was a wind. Lucy decided to hide deep among the coats, so she put out her hand to feel for the back of the wardrobe. It seemed to be a very big wardrobe and Lucy had to really stretch and stretch and then she felt something …

"Ouch!"

Lucy frowned. That was strange – she had touched something prickly. Why would there be something prickly in the wardrobe?

She took a step forward. Crunch.

What was that? Lucy wondered. Feeling suddenly, strangely colder, she crunched through the darkness. Lucy couldn't believe how big the wardrobe was and how cold and how prickly the coats were. Ahead of her, there was a tiny dot of very bright light. Lucy took another step into the impossibly big wardrobe. Slowly, the darkness around her lifted and everything was bathed in light. Then Lucy saw that the coat she had been touching was no coat at all but a green tree branch. She was standing in a forest…and it was snowing. There was a lamppost in the clearing in front of her.

Something crunched in the snow behind Lucy. She turned quickly and saw a very strange creature – he had legs like a goat, and two horns growing out of a thick patch of curly hair on his head. He was wearing a red scarf and carried an umbrella in one hand, and a bunch of packages wrapped in brown paper in the other.

The creature and Lucy let out a scream at the same time. The goat-man hopped behind a tree. Lucy was frightened, but she didn't know what to do.

"Are you hiding from me?" Lucy asked.

The creature peeped out from behind the tree. "No…" he said slowly, "I was just… I didn't want to scare you."

"If you don't mind me asking… what are you?" Lucy said, although she knew the creature was more frightened than she was.

"I'm a faun! What about you? Some kind of beardless dwarf?" the goat-man said.

Lucy laughed. "I'm not a dwarf," she told him. "I'm a girl!"

The creature gaped at her. "But you're human?"

"Of course," Lucy said.

The creature glanced around nervously as though he was expecting someone to arrive.

"I'm sorry. Allow me to introduce myself. My name is Tumnus."

"Pleased to meet you Mr Tumnus. I'm Lucy Pevensie." Lucy thought to herself that Fauns weren't real, but she didn't want to upset Mr Tumnus so she kept quiet and, after all, for an imaginary creature, he did seem very friendly.

"Well then, Lucy Pevensie… how would it be if you came and had tea with me?" asked the Faun shyly.

Lucy told Mr Tumnus that she ought to be getting back, but he wouldn't take no for an answer. "We'll have a roaring fire," he promised, "and toast, and hot tea, and cake."

Chapter Two

Lucy giggled. That did all sound lovely and secretly she didn't want to go back to the Professor's boring house just yet. This was lots more fun.

Mr Tumnus led Lucy through the wintry landscape, out of the forest, down a slope and across a plain. They arrived at Mr Tumnus' house. It was small, made of rock and set next to some tall cliffs – almost like a cave. It was surprisingly warm and cosy inside.

Once inside, Mr Tumnus explained to Lucy that this place was Narnia. And that it was always winter and never Christmas. That seemed terribly sad to Lucy. Mr Tumnus himself seemed sad, underneath his smiles and kind eyes. "Of course he is sad," she thought. "There has been 100 years of winter and no Christmas."

Mr Tumnus gave Lucy toast and sardines. The food warmed her insides and the roaring fire warmed her outsides. Lucy felt happier and more comfortable than she had done since leaving her mother on the train platform back in London … she also felt very tired. Mr Tumnus produced a strange looking musical instrument and began to play the most peculiar and beautiful music Lucy had ever heard in her life. As her eyes began to close, Lucy thought she saw creatures in the fire. Magical creatures! There were Dwarfs feasting, Nymphs dancing and, just as she drifted off to sleep, Lucy thought she heard the roar of a mighty lion.

Lucy awoke with a start. Perhaps only a few seconds had passed, yet the fire had gone out and the whole house suddenly seemed strangely cold. Mr Tumnus himself had turned very pale.

"I should be going," said Lucy.

"I'm such a terrible faun," replied Mr Tumnus. Lucy didn't like this reply. She couldn't understand it.

"You can't have done anything that bad," Lucy said, trying to sound kind and jolly and

handing him her handkerchief to dry his eyes.

"It isn't something I have done, Lucy Pevensie," said the Faun, turning to Lucy with cold, frightened eyes, "It's something I am doing."

Mr Tumnus' words made Lucy's heart sink. He was scaring her. His house didn't seem nice and cosy any more. It seemed like a prison.

"What are you doing?" Lucy stuttered, as fear grew in her belly.

Mr Tumnus looked at her and then said three very scary words indeed.

"I'm kidnapping you."

Lucy was frightened and wanted to be back with her brothers and sister. But Mr Tumnus wouldn't let her go. He said that he had to keep her there by order of the White Witch! "She's the one who makes it always winter," Mr Tumnus explained, "If we ever find a human in the woods, we're supposed to turn it over to her."

Now Lucy understood why Mr Tumnus had seemed so sad and nervous … if he didn't do what the White Witch ordered he would be turned to stone.

Lucy's face trembled. "I thought you were my friend."

Mr Tumnus looked down and saw in his hand Lucy's handkerchief that she had given him. A change came over his face; he looked full of strength and goodness.

They had to move quickly and quietly, as Mr Tumnus said, "the whole wood is full of her spies. Even some of the trees are on her side." They ran back across the plain, back up the slope and back through the forest until … with relief they saw the lamppost.

Mr Tumnus began to cry as he said goodbye to Lucy. In his heart, he was a very good creature and was ashamed at the evil deed he had nearly done. Lucy gave Mr Tumnus her handkerchief as a sign of their friendship. The kind Faun cried even more.

"No matter what happens, Lucy Pevensie," Mr Tumnus said, "I'm glad to have met you. You've made me feel warmer than I've felt in a hundred years."

Lucy turned and pushed on through the pine trees until their bristles became soft and she was finally back in the wardrobe among the fur coats. She tumbled out and rushed through the door. She thought about how long she had been away and how worried Peter and Susan would be.

Lucy burst into the corridor and shouted, "It's all right! I'm back!"

Edmund poked his head out from behind the velvet curtain and sneered at Lucy.

"Shut up".

This wasn't the welcome that Lucy had expected. They couldn't still be playing hide and seek! Surely she had been gone for hours?

Peter and Susan appeared.

"Weren't you wondering where I was?" Lucy asked. She tried to explain that she had been gone for hours, but the other three looked confused.

It was very strange. For Peter, Susan and Edmund, not one minute nor even one second had passed all the time that Lucy had been in Narnia.

Lucy told them about the magical land and about Mr Tumnus' house, but rather than being excited, they didn't believe her. So she dragged them to the wardrobe. Putting her hand between the coats, Susan knocked the back of the wardrobe. It was solid wood.

"One game at a time, Lu. We don't all have your imagination," said Peter.

It didn't seem fair. Then, Edmund spoke up.

"I believe you," he said, and Lucy's heart soared. "Didn't I tell you about the football field in the bathroom cupboard?" Edmund then grinned a nasty grin. This was too much for Lucy to bear. It was bad enough that Narnia and Mr Tumnus had disappeared and that no one would believe her story ... but to be laughed at! She ran from the room.

Lucy was still upset as she lay in her horrible, scratchy bed that night, unable to sleep. She knew the others thought that she was lying... but Narnia was real. But, if it was real, why wasn't it there when the others opened the wardrobe?

Lucy decided she had to have another look.

Quietly, she crept out of bed and down the hall to the wardrobe room. As she opened the door to the wardrobe, a cold gust of wind blew against her face. Narnia!

Lucy stepped inside and felt the familiar snow under her feet. She had to see if Mr Tumnus was safe or if the White Witch had heard of Lucy's visit and had punished the good Faun. She ran through the snow and didn't stop running until she reached Mr Tumnus' door.

Mr Tumnus was safe and well. No one had discovered his secret, that he was now firm friends with a human. They drank tea and shared more stories about Narnia and about Lucy's home and family. Lucy wanted to stay with Mr Tumnus for a long time; he was much kinder to her then her brothers and sister, particularly Edmund. However, it was not safe for her to stay too long and so, after saying a very happy goodbye to her Faun friend, Lucy ran back to the lamppost. But there she got a very big and pleasant surprise … "Edmund!" Her brother Edmund was in Narnia. Now, Peter and Susan would have to believe that it was a real place. As Lucy ran up to Edmund, she thought that he looked a little sick. "I'm freezing," he grumbled. "How do we get out of here?"

In a flash, Lucy had dragged Edmund back through the wardrobe and out of Narnia. She

was so excited that her feet barely touched the ground as she rushed into Peter and Susan's bedroom.

"Peter, Peter, wake up! It's there, it's really there!" she shouted as she jumped on Peter's bed. She was so pleased that she could prove her story about Narnia was true. "And this time, Edmund went too!" she said. This was going to be wonderful, thought Lucy. They would be able to have adventures, and all visit Mr Tumnus and explore Narnia properly and …

"You know how little children are," Edmund said, with a nasty grin on his face. "They just don't know when to stop pretending."

It seemed that the whole world crumbled and crashed. She cried with more sadness than she had ever cried in her life. Edmund had betrayed her, but why? She wanted to get away from her brothers and sisters and ran out the room, turned a corner and, still sobbing, bumped into something very big … it was a tall, grey haired man.

It was the Professor!

Chapter Three

Lucy sat glumly in the shade of a tree, brushing her doll's hair. A little distance away, her brothers and sister were playing cricket. She didn't want to play. She didn't even want to talk to them. They had all been very unpleasant to her, especially Edmund. The only people who were nice to her any more were Mr Tumnus and the Professor. The Professor hadn't been cross with her when she ran into him last night. Neither had he teased her about Narnia. It seemed wrong to her that strangers should treat her more kindly than her own family. Maybe the Professor knew about Narnia, after all it was his wardrobe and …

CRASH! SMASH! CLANG!

Lucy's thoughts were interrupted by a loud crashing sound. The boys had knocked a cricket ball through one of the Professor's windows. Inside, the library carpet was covered in glass, and a suit of armour lay across the floor.

They heard Mrs Macready coming, and ran through the house, looking for a hiding place. But every direction they turned, they could hear her footsteps. Finally, there was only one place left … the wardrobe.

Peter opened the door to the wardrobe. They scrambled inside. Lucy felt the familiar gust of cold air and saw the magical glow of light … but her brothers and sisters hadn't noticed it yet. She listened with a big smile on her face as Susan asked in a confused voice, "Peter, are your trousers wet?"

All four children were sitting in snow. They were in Narnia. Lucy found Susan's surprise very funny.

"Don't worry," Lucy said. "I'm sure it's just your imagination."

Peter and Susan were very embarrassed at the fact that they hadn't believed Lucy and had thought she was telling lies. Peter was also angry with Edmund and forced him to apologise. But Lucy wasn't interested in that; she had already forgiven her family. Besides, she was far too pleased at having this chance to introduce them to Mr Tumnus to worry about anything else. This was going to be the best visit to Narnia yet, she thought, as now she had her brothers and sister to share it with her.

Lucy led them to the funny stone house. But then she saw something that struck a very cold fear into her heart … the door to Mr Tumnus' house had been torn off its hinges.

"Who would do something like this?" Lucy asked. Her voice was shaking and tears were running down her face.

Mr Tumnus' house was in a terrible mess. Everything was smashed. Every teacup was broken. Worst of all though, Mr Tumnus was missing. Peter read a note he found,

"The faun Tumnus is hereby charged with High Treason against her Imperial Majesty Jadis, Queen of Narnia for comforting her enemies and fraternising with Humans. Signed Maugrim, Captain of the Secret Police"

"I'm the human!" said Lucy. "She must have found out he helped me." Lucy knew who this Queen was. She wasn't a real Queen at all. She was the evil White Witch. Susan wanted to go home, but Lucy refused. She couldn't let Mr Tumnus suffer for helping her. He was a kind creature and needed their help. Lucy told her brothers and sister that they had to stop the White Witch from turning Mr Tumnus to stone.

"But how?" thought Lucy.

"Psst!"

The Pevensies looked at one another, then peered out the door. A very large beaver crooked a finger at them.

"Psst! Lucy Pevensie?" the Beaver asked. He held out his hand and there was something Lucy recognised … it was her handkerchief, the one she had given to Mr Tumnus.

"Is he all right?" Lucy asked.

The Beaver looked around nervously. "That's better left for safer quarters." Suddenly, he turned and hurried off. Lucy and the others followed him. All Lucy could think about was that Mr Tumnus was in danger because of her. But how had the White Witch found out about her visits?

The Beaver lived with Mrs Beaver in a large dam on a frozen river. Although it was cold outside, it was warm and friendly inside. But what about Mr Tumnus?

"They'll have taken him to the Witch's house and there's few go through those gates who ever come out." Mr Beaver shook his head. Lucy began to weep. Mrs Beaver told her not to worry and then Mr Beaver grandly announced, "Aslan is on the move."

Lucy had never heard of Aslan before, but whoever he was, the very mention of his name gave her a feeling of great joy.

Mr Beaver was surprised that they did not know who Aslan was.

"He's the real king of Narnia! He's back and he's waiting for you at the Stone Table," Mr Beaver said. And then he repeated an old prophecy of Narnia.

"When Adam's flesh and Adam's bone,
  Sits at Cair Paravel in throne,
  The evil time will be over and done."

The Beavers explained this meant that when two boys and two girls arrive in Narnia, the children and Aslan would defeat the White Witch and restore peace to Narnia.

Lucy played the name Aslan around in her head. The very sound itself was wonderful. She was excited about going to the Stone Table and was ready for the adventure, as long as she had her brothers and sister with her.

But she didn't.

Edmund had vanished.

In the frigid night, they followed Edmund's footprints as they trailed off between two hills. Soon, the reason why became apparent. A sinister castle rose up in the distance and poor Edmund was making his way through the castle gates.

"Edmund!" Lucy cried.

"Shhh!" implored Mr. Beaver. "They'll hear you!"

"We can't just let him go," Susan shot back.

"He's our brother!" added Lucy.

Suddenly, Lucy understood. That was what Edmund had been doing during her second visit to Mr Tumnus and that was why he looked so sickly and had been so cruel to her by lying to the others.

"Only Aslan can help your brother now,"

Mr Beaver said. That settled it. Peter, Susan and Lucy were going to the Stone Table, no matter how dangerous it might be. The quest for Aslan had begun.

Mrs Beaver packed in a panic. They needed food for the long journey ahead. A piercing howl cut through the night air. It seemed to cut all the way into Lucy's soul. There was a second howl. Then a third … a fourth … Lucy looked at Peter and Susan. The air was alive with terrifying wolf cries. It was the Witch's secret police. There was no time to waste.

"Hurry, Mother, They're after us!" said Mr Beaver and pulled aside a cupboard to reveal a hidden tunnel.

The tunnel was dark, damp and very frightening. Lucy realised that she needed to brave. Not just for her sake, but for the sake of Mr Tumnus and Edmund. All she had to reassure her was the name Aslan, but it seemed to work. She heard a growling behind her.

"They're in the tunnel."

The secret police were getting closer and closer. Lucy thought that she could feel their foul breath on the back of her neck. Finally, they exited the tunnel and popped up near a village full of the Beavers' friends. Lucy was pleased to see squirrel children playing in the street. But something was wrong with the way they were playing. It was too slow … no, that wasn't it … they weren't moving at all!

The whole village had been turned to stone. Now, they were doomed. Mr Beaver kneeled, distraught.

"What happened here?" asked Peter.

"This is what becomes of those who cross the Witch," said a sly and unfamiliar voice. It was a fox accompanied by two satyrs.

"Take one more step and I'll chew you to splinters," growled Mr Beaver.

"Relax," soothed the Fox. "I'm one of the good guys."

The children were not sure whether or not to trust the newcomer. However, they had no choice and climbed up a large tree as the Satyrs ran off into the woods. Just as Lucy lifted her leg up into the safety of the branches, the wolves rushed out of the tunnel and into the village. Lucy was scared. Would the Fox keep his word?

"We're looking for some humans," said the largest wolf. Mr Tumnus had told Lucy about him. He was Maugrim, captain of the secret police.

"I imagine there'd be at least a nominal reward for something like that," replied the Fox. A second wolf violently grabbed the Fox by the neck. Lucy nearly screamed, but luckily Susan put her hand over her mouth.

"Your reward is your life." snarled Maugrim.

The Fox extended his paw. "Oh no," Lucy thought, "It looks like he's about to point this way."

Chapter Four

Lucy watched with terror as the Fox raised his paw and pointed ... North. With a vicious howl, the wolves shot off into the woods. Lucy was so relieved. They were safe. For the time being. Lucy thanked the Fox. "It has been a pleasure my Queen, and an honour." he replied. Lucy thought it was very odd that everyone thought her family were Kings and Queens of Narnia.

"I must gather my men. Your Majesties will need every hoof and claw in your war against the Witch," said the Fox. Mr and Mrs Beaver explained that, in order for them to reach the Stone Table in time, they would have to cross the Great River. This was the largest river in Narnia, but because of the 100 years of winter, it was completely frozen and safe to walk across.

Lucy hadn't realised that Narnia was big enough to have more than one river. After all, if a land fits inside a wardrobe, how big can it be?

"It's enormous," gasped Lucy. She was standing on a rock bridge looking across at all of Narnia. She became very worried about whether they would ever make it to the Stone

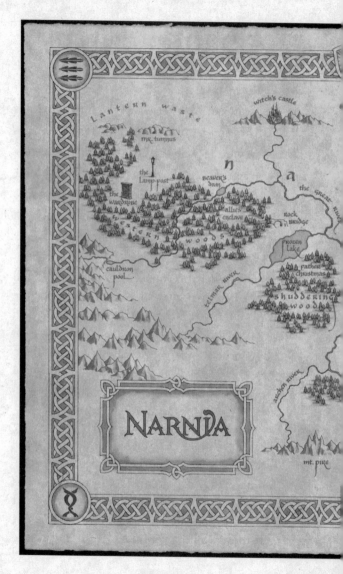

Table and Aslan; it seemed an impossibly long journey.

"Aslan's camp should be near the Stone Table, just across the great river," said Mrs Beaver in a cheerful voice.

Lucy, Susan, and Peter looked out at the hill. To Lucy, it seemed very small and far away.

They trudged forward through the snow.

And trudged … and trudged … and trudged … and nothing seemed to change as far as Lucy could tell. The hill stayed a long way away and Mr Beaver kept shouting back at the Pevensies, telling them to hurry up. Lucy thought that if she walked much further, her legs might fall off. Then something did change. Mr Beaver's jolly cries of 'hurry up' became full of fear.

"Run! Run!" he called in a panic.

Lucy heard a sharp rattle in the air … sleigh bells. She turned and saw gigantic, white plumes of snow heading towards them. It must be the White Witch. Lucy ran as fast as she could; her brother Peter grabbed her hand and held it tight. The Beavers had found a hiding hole and were waving to the children for them to run faster. Lucy thought she was going to collapse, then she remembered the goal of their journey, Aslan! The name filled her with strength and she sped up. They all dived into the hole and waited …

Lucy could hear the sounds of the sleigh. It was drawing closer. Then … nothing.

"Maybe she's gone," suggested Lucy. Mr Beaver bravely went to look. After a few minutes, he reappeared. "There's someone here to see you," he said, smiling.

Peeking out of the hole, Lucy saw a tall man with a long white beard wearing a brilliant red robe. He wore a sword at his hip. Lucy grinned. "Merry Christmas, sir," she said.

Father Christmas smiled at her. "It certainly is, Lucy, now that you've arrived."

"At last," thought Lucy happily, "Christmas has come to Narnia."

Father Christmas explained, "The hope that you have brought us, your majesties, is finally weakening the Witch's magic." Then his smile faded as he pulled a sack from his sleigh. "Still… You could probably do with these…"

"Presents!" Lucy cried.

Father Christmas handed Lucy a precious glass tube filled with a liquid.

"The juice of the fire flower," he explained, "one drop will cure any injury." He also gave Lucy a tiny dagger. Lucy thought that these were very unusual Christmas presents … but then this was a very unusual Christmas. She looked at the weapon and the glass vial and realised that, before this was over, she and her family may have to fight for their lives. "Long live Aslan," announced

Father Christmas. "And Merry Christmas!" And then he rode away.

Lucy smiled at the departing figure on his beautiful sleigh. She had always known in her heart that Father Christmas was real. And now she knew it to be true.

They pushed through the forest. With every step, the air seemed to get warmer. Soon, Lucy realised that the snow at her feet was turning to slush. Suddenly, they came upon a cherry tree in full flower. Peter picked up a petal.

"He said winter was almost over… you know what that means?" Peter said gravely.

"It means it's spring!" replied Lucy.

She couldn't understand why Peter wasn't pleased. Spring meant that the White Witch's magic was weakening. Then Lucy realised … spring would also mean that the ice on the Great River would be melting.

Many more long hours of walking finally led Lucy, Susan and Peter to the banks of the Great River. Cracks had formed along the ice, and dark water swirled below. Somewhere in the distance, they heard the howl of a wolf. They had to cross the river as quickly as they could.

Lucy stayed close to Peter as they hurried on the ice. Although Peter didn't seem to think that he could protect them, Lucy believed in him. Just

being near her elder brother made her feel safe. The ice cracked all around them as they walked and jets of freezing cold water flew up into the air. It was dangerous but they were nearly across and Lucy thought they were sure to make it to the other side safely when … Maugrim and another wolf dropped down in front of the children, blocking their way.

Lucy felt Peter's hand on her shoulder. He stepped forward and drew his sword. Maugrim began to tease Peter, while the other wolf pinned down Mr Beaver.

"Put that down, boy," Maugrim taunted. "Someone could get hurt. All my Queen wants is for you to take your family and go."

Susan thought that Peter should listen to him, but Lucy didn't. Peter looked very frightened. Lucy realised that although he was her elder brother, he was still not an adult. Maybe they ought to give in and go home … but deep inside of Lucy she was sure that Peter had the power to fight for good.

Peter lowered his sword, about to give up – but at that moment, a huge chunk of ice fell from the top of the nearby waterfall, cracking the river's surface. Before she knew what had happened, she was being held tightly in Peter's arm. With a quick stroke, Peter drove his sword into the surface of the ice. Lucy saw that all Peter's nervousness had vanished; he knew what he was doing.

CRACK!

The waterfall burst and the piece of ice that Lucy, Peter and Susan were standing on broke off. Lucy had never felt water so fierce, so powerful and so cold. It hurt to keep her eyes open. She saw the two wolves being dragged down the river, she saw the two Beavers swimming to safety and she saw Peter holding onto his sword for dear life ... for all three of their lives.

Then, there was a roar of water like a lion's roar and everything went dark and cold and quiet.

Chapter Five

At first, Peter and Susan could not see where Lucy had gone under the water. After a long, painful moment, Peter heard someone coughing on the shore – it was Lucy stumbling up the bank.

Back on dry land, Susan was angry and upset. She didn't believe in Aslan and wanted to return home. While Susan and Mr Beaver argued, Mrs Beaver noticed something wonderful happening. A solitary cherry tree was blossoming… Narnia was exploding into its first spring for 100 years!

Lucy felt as though she couldn't take another step. Although the air was sweet with the smell of flowers, her head ached, her legs ached, her arms ached … In fact, every part of her body ached. She lifted her head to ask Mr Beaver how much further it was and then she saw the Stone Table, rising up against the sky. They had made it. They had reached Aslan.

At the foot of the hill, was a camp of tents and flags stretching as far as Lucy could see. It was Aslan's army. And it was very big indeed.

The Beavers and the children hurried down to Aslan's camp, which was swarming with all sorts of creatures. Lucy saw centaurs and naiads and dryads and fauns like Mr Tumnus. It was like being inside a fairytale. Everyone stopped and made way for them. Finally, they came to a tent. Aslan's tent, thought Lucy.

Lucy gasped as an enormous, beautiful lion stepped out of the tent. In her eyes, he seemed to burn like a sun. The world was brighter and warmer for his presence. She knew, without being told, that this was Aslan – the rightful king of Narnia.

"Welcome, Peter, Son of Adam," Aslan said in his deep, rich voice. "Welcome, Susan and Lucy,

Daughters of Eve." Lucy felt giddy when Aslan spoke her name. "But where is the fourth?"

Peter explained that Edmund had fallen under the Witch's spell and had betrayed them. Lucy was worried that the mighty King might be angry with Edmund, but she needn't have worried. Aslan asked gently, "if this is true, then why does he deserve our help?"

Peter and Susan explained that they had both been too hard on Edmund, but Lucy had the simplest answer, "he's our brother." On hearing this, Aslan stared deep into her eyes. It felt to Lucy as though he was actually inside her or that she was inside him. He could sense her worry and she could sense his power and glory.

"All shall be done for Edmund," Aslan promised. "But it may be harder than you think."

"Oh, come on, try it on," Lucy and Susan were trying on Narnian gowns by the river. It was their first chance to rest since they had entered Narnia. Lucy splashed her sister and Susan splashed back and laughed loudly. Lucy was pleased that Susan had finally come to love this new world. In fact, Lucy thought that she hadn't heard Susan laugh properly for a very long time. Since Daddy went to war. It was a nice strong laugh, but there was something else in it … was it … a growl?

No! The growl was not Susan. It was Maugrim and another wolf. Susan swiftly blew her horn and then she and Lucy quickly climbed a tree to escape the wolves.

Within moments, Peter and Aslan arrived. Lucy and Susan watched as Peter confronted Maugrim again. Susan was very nervous, but Lucy reassured her. She had great faith in Peter, especially now that they had found Aslan. She knew that Peter would be victorious.

The wolf leapt. He and Peter fell to the ground…and lay perfectly still. Then Peter shoved Maugrim away. The wolf was dead. Aslan knighted Peter for his bravery. Lucy glowed with pride.

It was official; her brother was a hero!

When Lucy and Susan stumbled out of their tent the next morning, they saw that Peter was already awake – and staring out over the ridge. Lucy followed his gaze – and saw a boy walking alone with Aslan.

"Edmund!" Lucy cried. She was so pleased; Aslan's Centaurs had rescued him. Lucy couldn't take her eyes off him. It was if he had been gone from them for years and years.

She was still watching him happily when they sat down to have breakfast. Her happiness was shattered when Peter said that he wanted the others to go home now, before the battle, while he stayed to fight. That didn't seem right to Lucy. She felt that they had a duty to fight for Narnia. Lucy knew that she could not rest until she saw that Mr Tumnus was safe again. To her surprise, Edmund stood up and insisted that they all stay.

Lucy was helping Susan practise with her bow and arrow. "My big sister's aim is definitely improving," thought Lucy, as she watched the arrows strike close to the bull's-eye. It didn't look too hard actually. Lucy had a little go … and her dagger struck the target right in the centre.

Shortly they were interrupted by Mr Beaver shouting, "The Witch has demanded a meeting with Aslan."

Lucy watched with horror as the Witch approached. She had never actually seen her before. Although the Witch was tall and beautiful, there was something very cold and cruel about her. She looked as cool as ice, but as hard as rock.

"You have a traitor amongst you, Aslan," she declared in a sharp voice. "Every traitor belongs to me. His blood is my property." Lucy gasped. The White Witch was talking about Edmund and wanted to take him away. Lucy knew that Aslan would save her brother, but she was rather shocked when the Great Lion replied that the Witch was speaking the truth.

"How can it be right to give Edmund to her?" cried Lucy. "You said you'd help him!"

Aslan walked apart with the Witch. Lucy was devastated. She couldn't believe that Aslan would give Edmund back to the Witch. Surely, he couldn't do that …

After talking for some time, Aslan and the Witch returned and Aslan announced, "she has renounced her claim on your brother's blood."

Lucy felt a great relief. Edmund was saved and Aslan was true to his word. All of Aslan's camp cheered as the Witch left and Peter and Susan hugged Edmund. Only two people weren't cheering. Aslan, with a sad look, walked towards his tent and Lucy quietly watched him. Something was wrong.

Something was definitely wrong. Lucy could not sleep, and it wasn't because of Susan's snoring. She kept thinking about how sad Aslan had looked earlier. What was it that he had said to the Witch that made her change her mind? Lucy was thinking so much about the mighty King that she even imagined him walking past her tent and out into the night …

Lucy rubbed her eyes. It wasn't her imagination. Aslan was leaving. She woke her sister quickly and the pair of them silently followed the wonderful beast.

To Lucy, Aslan looked as though someone had taken all of his power and strength. His head hung low and he padded slowly towards the Stone Table with a very sad air. Aslan allowed them to follow but insisted that they could not come with him all the way. Just before they reached the top of the hill where the Stone Table stood, Aslan asked Lucy and

Susan to stop walking with him. He thanked the two girls and said farewell. Lucy couldn't understand what was happening. Aslan was talking as though he was never going to see them again.

Chapter Six

Lucy and Susan hid in the bushes as the Lion trudged heavily to the Stone Table. They saw a terrible sight – a crowd of horrible creatures waited for him. There were Ogres and Hags, Minotaurs and Goblins – and at the end of the table…the White Witch.

The Witch grinned. "Behold," she said with a sneer, "the Great Lion."

Aslan did not protest as the creatures rushed at him, knocking him onto his back and tying his paws.

"Why doesn't he fight back?" Lucy whispered to her sister. It didn't make any sense. Aslan was powerful enough to defeat all of these monsters. Yet he would not fight. It was the worst thing that Lucy had ever seen, as the beautiful Lion was tortured and beaten, and had all his marvellous golden fur cruelly shaved off. Then the Witch raised a magical stone knife high.

"Please," thought Lucy, "please Aslan … save yourself." At that moment, Aslan turned his eyes from the sky and looked straight at Lucy.

She couldn't watch and hugged her sister out of fear. She heard the knife fall. There was a terrible thud and then … the White Witch's icy, cruel voice cried out, "the Great Cat is dead!"

It was quiet at the Stone Table now. The Witch and her monstrous army had gone to prepare for the battle tomorrow. Only Susan and Lucy … and the dead Aslan remained.

Lucy thought that perhaps her fire flower potion could save him, but it was too late. He was dead and his body was as cold as the White Witch's evil stare.

"He must have known what he was doing…" Susan said as she looked at the Lion's lifeless face.

Lucy wrapped her arms around Susan, and the sisters cried as though their hearts would never be mended.

They continued to cry and hug until the sun came up. The light danced across the motionless Lion.

"He looks better in the light, doesn't he?" said Lucy hopefully. She and Susan knew that Peter would be getting the army ready and that they ought to go back and help. They began to walk away when they heard a low rumble and a sudden noise like thunder. Lucy felt the whole world shake and fell to the floor.

When she stood up, she was shocked to see the Stone Table was cracked in two and Aslan had disappeared.

"Is this more magic?" Susan asked.

"Yes. It is more magic!" replied a low voice. Lucy recognised it immediately, but how was it possible? She turned and there … was Aslan. Not only was he not dead, but he also seemed more powerful and splendid than ever before.

"The Witch has learned the Deep magic well. But if she could have looked back further, into the stillness before the dawn of time, she would have seen there was a different incantation. That when a willing victim who has committed no treachery is killed in the traitor's stead… the Table would crack and even death itself would start working backwards," proclaimed Aslan and then he gave a mighty roar. The roar was so strong that Lucy thought it must surely fill the whole of Narnia.

Lucy laughed almost as loudly as Susan screamed. They were riding on Aslan's back as he leapt across the countryside. He was rushing to the White Witch's castle. Lucy didn't think that anything could travel so fast.

When they reached the castle, they were confronted with a horrible sight. Statues. There were statues everywhere. Statues that had once been living, breathing creatures. Lucy stopped in her tracks. She couldn't breathe. In front of her was Mr Tumnus, frozen in cold, dead stone. Lucy was too late to save her friend … yet, she believed in Aslan. If his magic was more powerful than the Witch's, could he save her friend?

Aslan leaned forward and breathed on Mr Tumnus' face. Although the White Witch's magic was cold and terrible, the Lion's breath was warm and life-giving. A glow spread across Mr Tumnus and then he spoke … "Lucy Pevensie."

Lucy hugged her friend. He was alive! And, in only a few moments, so were all the other creatures that the Witch had turned into statues.

Lucy stood with Aslan, Susan, Mr Tumnus and many, many more creatures and looked at the battlefield below. Aslan's army, under Peter's command, had fought well, but the Witch's forces were stronger. Lucy knew that Aslan could turn the tide of the battle … and so he did. She watched with pride as the fierce creature jumped into the fight. All the cowardly monsters in the Witch's army who had so meanly beaten Aslan when he was tied up were now unwilling to fight and fled from him in fear.

Lucy cheered as she saw Aslan pounce onto the Witch. She was defeated and her army was fleeing. Lucy could see her brother Peter, but…

"Where is Edmund?" she asked.

He was lying on the ground. His eyes were closed and half of the Witch's wand was sticking out of his body.

He had saved Peter from the White Witch, but had been seriously injured. He looked like he was dying. Lucy did not despair. She had seen Aslan return from the dead and save those that she had thought lost. Lucy knew that she had the power to save Edmund; she had the fire flower liquid.

With great love and attention, she tipped the glass tube and sent one drop falling into Edmund's mouth. She hoped with all her heart that it would heal him. It did! He was alive and saved. Lucy then moved around the battlefield healing all the wounded creatures.

As she did so, she looked around. Her brothers and sister were alive. Mr Tumnus was rescued. Narnia was saved. All her wishes had come true …

It still felt too good to be true, even when Mr Tumnus pinned a silver laurel to her hair and she and her family sat in the four beautiful thrones at Cair Paravel.

As the celebration carried on throughout the day, Lucy spied a familiar golden figure silently slipping outside. She rushed to the balcony and watched as Aslan strode away along the seashore… away from Cair Paravel.

"Is he coming back?" she asked Mr Tumnus, who had quietly joined her.

"In time," he replied. "But you mustn't press him."

Lucy tried to feel better. "After all, he's not a tame lion, is he?"

"No," Mr Tumnus smiled. "But he is good."

"The White Stag makes wishes come true," explained King Peter to Queen Lucy. King Edmund and Queen Susan rode behind them. It was many years since the battle against the White Witch and the two Kings and two Queens of Narnia were chasing through the forest, hunting the White Stag.

Queen Lucy wasn't very interested in the White Stag. She didn't have any wishes she wanted to come true … except that she had been recently dreaming about another world and about a lovely woman who she missed very much … a mother?

All four monarchs reached a clearing in the woods and saw a very unusual sight … it was a metal tree with a light at the top. For some reason, it seemed familiar to Queen Lucy. Then she remembered. It was here that she had first met her good friend Mr Tumnus. But where had she come from … where had they all come from?

They all got off their horses and walked into the dense forest. There was a smell that Queen Lucy thought she hadn't smelt since she was a little girl of eight. It was a smell … of mothballs!

The wood had disappeared and the trees had turned into fur coats and suddenly … THUMP!

Lucy fell out of the wardrobe and landed on her brother Edmund. Peter and Susan were underneath him. They were children once again!

The door to the room opened and in walked Professor Kirke. Not one minute had passed since the four Pevensies had entered Narnia. Lucy remembered where she was … she was back in England.

It was late at night and nothing was stirring in Professor Kirke's house. Nothing, except young Lucy Pevensie. She was standing before the large wardrobe, alone. She took a deep breath, opened the door and … coats. There was nothing but coats.

"I'm afraid you won't get back in that way," said a kind voice. It was Professor Kirke.

"Will we ever go back?" Lucy asked.

"Oh my, yes," said the Professor with a smile. "Best to keep your eyes open."

Lucy smiled as well. She could fancy another adventure in Narnia one day. But not today.